Arthur Matthison, Emile Augier

A False Step

The prohibited play, freely adapted from Les lionnes pauvres

Arthur Matthison, Emile Augier

A False Step
The prohibited play, freely adapted from Les lionnes pauvres

ISBN/EAN: 9783337285999

Printed in Europe, USA, Canada, Australia, Japan

Cover: Foto ©Andreas Hilbeck / pixelio.de

More available books at **www.hansebooks.com**

*Dedicated to the True Censor of the British Stage—
The British Public.*

"A FALSE STEP:"

The Prohibited Play,

Freely adapted from " *Les Lionnes Pauvres,*"

BY

ARTHUR MATTHISON,

AUTHOR OF

" *The Little Hero*"; " *Il Talismano*"; " *Enoch Arden*" (*a
Drama*); " *Liz*" (*in collaboration with Joseph Hatton*);
" *Contempt of Court*; *etc. etc.,*

LONDON:
SAMUEL FRENCH,
PUBLISHER,
89, STRAND.

NEW YORK:
SAMUEL FRENCH & SON,
PUBLISHERS.
38, EAST 14TH STREET.

Characters.

Mr. Prendergast (*a Solicitor*) ... ...

  „ Alfred Duval (*a Barrister*) ... ...

  „ Fred Livingstone (*a Man of the World*) ...

  „ Job Gosling (*a Retired Poulterer*)... ...

Young Mr. Greenway ... ...

John ... ...

Guests ... ...

Mrs. Duval ... ...

Mrs. Prendergast ... ...

Mrs. George Reynolds ... ...

Miss Amanda Gosling ... ...

Madame Angélique ... ...

Charlotte ... ...

TIME—PRESENT.

CORRESPONDENCE on "A FALSE STEP."

From the "Times" of Oct. 2nd.

A PROHIBITED PLAY.

TO THE EDITOR OF THE TIMES.

Sir,—Permit me to address you on a subject which may be called public, inasmuch as it concerns playgoers and all interested in matters theatric. A piece of mine entitled *A False Step* was in preparation at the Court Theatre, but has been proscribed by the Lord Chamberlain. I adapted it from *Les Lionnes Pauvres*, by Emile Augier, played in Paris, some years ago, with great success. The Examiner of Plays "feeling compelled, in the responsible exercise of a public duty, to reject the play," characterises it as "profoundly moral in its ultimate purpose," but fears that "if presented to a mixed English audience it would give much offence, and would scarcely be accepted as a satire on the prevailing manners and customs of English society"—by the way, "satire" is not the *mot of Les Lionnes Pauvres*, it is condemnation. The Examiner further thinks that "the public and their critical guides would exclaim at the 'situations' and say that the moral of the piece was only fit to be taught in the Divorce Court." He adds, in his letter to me, "It is not without reluctance and regret that I find myself obliged to reject a piece which has so much merit in it as your version of Augier's fine and powerful play."

I would fain know why a fine, powerful, and profoundly moral play should be thus condemned ; why my growing dramatic reputation should be thus unjustly injured ; and why a moral lesson may not be taught nightly on the stage, instead of only once in the Divorce Court? As to "situations," those in *A False Step* would blush to find themselves compared to many whose *immorale* has been freely "taught" to the public in stage plays any time these two years. For confirmation of this assertion I refer you to *Les Lionnes Pauvres* itself and to the several popular plays easy recognisable. In the play in question there is no adultery made easy. The cruelty, the anguish, the impolicy, even, of this particular falling away, are shewn so vividly, are so forcibly impressed upon the spectator ; the Nemesis at the end of the play is so stern, severe, and implacable, that no better moral lesson could be given by book, poem, stage, or pulpit. I am advised to publish *A False Step*, as the public may think it a thousand times stronger than it is, and I may consequently find great difficulties in obtaining a hearing for my future plays original or adapted.

It is very probable that I shall print it. In the meantime I pray you will allow the court of public opinion to hear me in my defence, so far as the present letter may speak for me.

I am, Sir, yours most respectfully,

Savage Club, Oct. 1.   ARTHUR MATTHISON.

From "The Era" of Oct. 13th.

A   PROHIBITED   PLAY

TO THE EDITOR OF THE ERA.

Sir,—As the discussion on *A False Step* is of general interest, I ask you to favour me by printing the enclosed correspondence between Mr. Clement Scott and myself upon the subject.

Yours most respectfully,

A. MATTHISON.

Savage Club, October 10th.

[COPY.]

"Savage Club, 5th October, 1878.

"My dear Clement Scott,—In a letter I deemed official, received by me from the Lord Chamberlain's Office, announcing that my play *A False Step* could not be recommended for licence occurs the folowing passage :—

"'But in the form of an adaptation to English life and society, and presented to a mixed English audience, I fear that it would give much offence. Our public *and their critical guides* would fasten on the 'situations,' which are extremely *scabreuses*, and would exclaim that the moral of the piece was only fit to be taught through the Divorce Court.'

"As you are one of the 'critical guides' of the public, and as I value your opinion, you would be doing me a personal favour by reading *A False Step*, and recording your impression on the moral and satirical points at issue.

"Yours faithfully,

"Clement Scott, Esq."   "ARTHUR MATTHISON."

[COPY.]

"Union Club, S.W., 8th October, 1878.

"My dear Arthur Matthison,—At your request I have read your play *A False Step* very carefully and very critically, and I cannot refrain from expressing my opinion on it at some length, and for two reasons—first, because common report and official action misled me entirely as to the general character of the work ; and, secondly, because I am anxious to try and break down, or at any rate to weaken, the fabric of that obstinate barrier of prejudice, or superficial reasoning, that deprives the English dramatist of his rights and privileges, as the journalist of the manners of his time, and the critic of the society of to-day. You are accused, as I am aware, of a certain hastiness in protesting against the opinions of those who are by law appointed to guide your pen into the paths of moral rectitude, and to determine for you and other educated authors of our time the limit of stage satire ; you are taunted with an indiscretion in publishing that which was intended for your private eye, and for alarming the world with what are called your 'private grievances ;' but being afflicted myself with the weaknesses of human nature, I can, at any rate, sympathise with a man who, acting up to his own conscience, and to his notion of right and wrong, is suddenly and summarily deprived of instant capital and the means of striving towards success. To refuse a play as one unworthy of representation in public, be the reason for the refusal what it may, is naturally to incur a very grave responsibility. Your censors' opinions are stifled ; the public mind is prejudiced ; and you, the author of the supposed indiscretion, have no Court of Appeal.

"Before I read your play, I, like the rest of the public, was naturally prejudiced against it, for I had the authority of those best competent to judge, that it was an unworthy satire and an unfair picture of English life. I was surprised ; but I put *A False Step* down in the catalogue of French obscenities that pass for wit. I naturally concluded it was worse than *La Marjolaine*, more gross than *Les Cent Vierges*, and more suggestive than a certain scene played by Chaumont [and exquisitely played] in *Madame attend Monsieur*. Many people dismissed your play, as I did, with something like a sneer. One correspondent, writing to the *Times*, held up his hands in an attitude of holy deliverance from another French play, and thought, as many other ignorant people think, that every French play is necessarily filthy. But what do I find when I come to read the play ? not a general satire on morals, but an absolute and accurate picture of English life as I see it, and as I believe it to be ; not a dressing-up of French characters in English clothes, but the husbands, the wives, the sins, the frivolities, the temptations, the weaknesses, the hollowness, the cant, and the veneer of England and English Society as I conceive it to exist in this age and at this time in which we live. I grant that the picture is painful ; it is none the less true. I allow that hundreds who know it to be true, and bitterly deplore it, would swear it was false, for this is an English failing, this horror of depreciation. I admit that people would get up from this play irritated and annoyed because none of us like to be told how weak, and sinful, and foolish we are. I confess that when I go to the play I prefer to be amused than to be preached at, and that I would far rather see portrayed the gentleness, the kindness, the beauty, and the tenderness of life, than sit in your dissecting-room whilst you skinned Society before my eyes. But until it is proved to me that the dramatist must not be the journalist; that the play-writer may not do what the leader-writer does every day in the week; that Society at large is under the protection of a high official, or that it is more immoral of a clever and most satirical writer to describe the weakness and the failings of Mr. and Mrs. Jack Spratt, in the columns of *Punch*, than it is for you to tell precisely the same kind of story with less satire and more truth, about your Prendergasts and Duvals on the stage ; then I am bound to declare, as I do now declare, with honesty and without hesitation, that I cannot conceive a story, more true to the failings of the Society of to-day, or characters so widely represented in the world we live in, than the one embodied in your play.   If it be immoral to hold up to public reprobation that Westbourne-grove school of life and manners that breeds frivolous children and foolish wives ; if it be immoral to heap our scorn upon the mothers who teach their children from their cradles to worship Mammon and to put money in their purses how they can, to be extravagant as girls and to be reckless as women ; if it be immoral to tell these thoughtless and ill-disciplined young ladies of this Victorian age that if they carry their pranks into married life they will ruin households and break hearts ;   if it be satirical to tell Society, what it knows already, that married women occasionally wear dresses that are not paid for by their husbands, and that married men make presents to women who are not their wives, then indeed, your play is both immoral and satirical to a fault.   I hear and appreciate the cry of anguish of your frivolous and tempted wife, Mrs. Prendergast, when she says, 'What could you expect of me ? Who ever taught me anything ? What was my own mother's maxim ? That to be happy you must be rich. What have I learned in the world ? That you must be rich to be thought anything of ! Pleasure and luxury, money, jewels, dresses are the gods I have been taught to worship both by word and example ; and because I do worship them, because I would have them, I am a monster ! Let it end ! I am tired of my false life !" And I recognise in this wail of the heroine in your banished play an echo, a positive echo of a lecture delivered the other day at the Mansion House on ' Extravagance,' by a clever woman (Miss Emily Faithfull) to her own sex, in the presence of Lord Shaftesbury and divines of the Established Church, and with the approbation of the thinking world !   But it is moral in the City, and immoral at the Court.   I seek high and low for immorality in your play, for risky scenes, for doubtful language, for equivocal talk, for un-English sentiment ; but I can find nothing.   It is painful, it is hideously true ; nothing more.   It may annoy society to find it is detected and pilloried, it may lessen the value of fashionable photographs in the shop windows, but it is true, all true, every word of it.   The weakness and folly of your Mrs. Prendergast, who throws dust in the eyes of her husband and deceives her best friend, are as true as the weakness and folly of Mrs. Jack Spratt, in *Punch*, who neglects her children and allows an old peer to ogle her at supper time. If your play is suppressed, then certain copies of comic and satirical publications ought to be burned by the common hangman ! Now, I am not likely—am I—to consider *Peril* an immoral work, nor do I think it is. Quite the contrary. But it was open to question on account of the ' physical ' means by which the moral was arrived at. The virtuous woman in *Peril* were certainly tempted, and the physical facts of her temptation was pretty strongly put before the audience. But in your play I cannot discover that there is any temptation at all. There is no chasing round tables and chairs, there is no pulling

down of bell ropes or calling for help, there is not even a single love
scene in the play, and, as far as I can understand it, your guilty heroine
was far more vain than vicious.   Pardon me if I misunderstand
your story, but this is how I should describe it if I had been per-
mitted to see it sitting in a stall at the Theatre. This is how I should
endeavour to place it before the public :— There are two married
couples living on terms of intimate friendship in London, a Mr. and
Mrs. Prendergast, and a Mr. and Mrs. Duval.   Mrs. Prendergast,
who has been a spoiled child from her infancy, selfish to the back-
bone, badly brought up, and taught to live for money, dress, and
extravagance, has married an elderly man who is too blindly fond
of her to see her faults or to check her frivolity.   Mrs. Duval, who
owes everything in life to her former guardian, old Prendergast, the
husband of her friend, has married a man she believes in, whom
she loves, but who plays her false.   Whilst old Prendergast is
slaving to support his wife, and Mrs. Duval is stinting herself
and denying herself every comfort for her husband's sake, this
very husband is spending all his income and more, borrowing
money and compromising himself in a hundred ways, blinded by
his infatuation for Mrs. Prendergast.   The treacherous intrigue between the married Duval and the married Mrs. Prendergast is un-
happily, if I am to believe the Divorce Court, not an uncommon
form of intrigue in English society.   There is nothing particularly
Parisian about it.   The milliners of Regent-street and Bond-street,
I daresay, could tell pretty much the same stories of how married
women's bills are paid as could Worth or Pingat, or Leferrier ; and,
doubtless, the tale has pretty much the same end in Paris as in
England.   This is surely no exaggerated picture, no Napoleonic
code of morals.   At last the guilty pair are unmasked, at last old
Prendergast discovers that he has been a doting, trusting fool, and
at last Mrs. Duval, in bitter tears and agony, knows that she has
wasted all her life, all her affection, and all her trust on a worthless
man.   But what is the moral ?   Not the moral of your Hennequins
and authors of that stamp, who laugh at virtue and applaud vice ;
not the moral of the modern French vaudeville, which makes us
roar with laughter at the eccentricity of the most vicious people—
certainly not.   What is the answer of the outraged Mrs. Duval, in
your scouted work, when her guilty and detested husband comes
blubbering and whining at the feet of his injured wife.   ' You have
sacrificed, and for ever, the true love of a true woman, and as loyal
a friendship as ever man gave to man !   Look at your work !—two
crushed lives and two broken households.   Never hope or think
to see me again ; our lives, as our hearts, are no longer one, for the
pr sent has killed the past.   Not a word more.   Leave time and me
to try and make your peace ! '   And then the curtain falls. I repeat,
my dear Matthison, that this is not a scene that Society will like, as at
present constituted.   Too many withers will be wrung ; but if such
scenes and such pictures are held to be immoral or too satirical for
the sensitive nature of an English audience, and if Society is to be
protected from exposure on the stage, then I repeat that the drama
and the dramatists of to-day are denied a privilege based on the

precedent of centuries ! I forbear to touch upon certain awkard-nesses in the ' form' of your play which I do not think would have escaped the attention of your critics. For the present I have con-tented myself with the 'colour.' It would have been more conve-nient to an audience if you could have told so slight a story in less than five acts, and I do not think—if you will pardon me for saying so—that you have thoroughly sifted from your dialogue all the husks and chaff of French idiom and expression. Such a subject was worth treating, in my opinion, from a more thoroughly English standpoint, and in a more English style. And now I have done. You will excuse me, I trust, for the freedom of my speech ; but after I had made myself acquainted with your work it did not seem loyal to an old friend and fellow-worker to withhold my emphatic belief that you have done nothing but what an earnest and conscientious dramatist would desire to do with a full sense of his responsibility to art and the public.

> " Yours faithfully,
> " CLEMENT SCOTT.

" Arthur Matthison, Esq."

A FALSE STEP.

ACT I.

An elegant parlour at MRS. PRENDERGAST'S. *Window at back; fire-place,* R. ; *doors,* R. *and* L. ; *doorway, with hangings,* L.

CHARLOTTE *discovered* ; MRS. DUVAL *entering.*

MRS. D. Your mistress is not at home, it seems.

CHAR. No, madame ; but I expect her directly.

MRS. D. And is Mr. Prendergast out also ?

CHAR. No, madame ; he is in his study. Here he comes ,

Exit CHARLOTTE, *as* PRENDERGAST *enters.* PRENDERGAST *and* MRS. DUVAL *salute cordially.*

MRS. D. You see, I make your house my home, as usual ; and am now come to wait for my husband, who promised to meet me here.

PREN. Glad to hear it. It seems months since I saw him.

MRS. D. Ah, you must not blame him. He is always so busy.

PREN. Glad to hear it. For one lawyer who works, there are a dozen who don't.

MRS. D. Cecilia is out, I find.

PREN. Yes ; she has gone to the riding-school.

MRS. D. To the riding-school !

PREN. Yes ; she takes her first lesson to-day, by the doctor's orders, my dear.

MRS. D. Is she ill ?

PREN. No, thank Heaven, but her health requires——

MRS. D. Amusement ?

PREN. Well, it really seems something like it, I confess, but what matter ? I see no great harm in Cecilia on horseback, unless indeed (*smiling*) she were to fall off.

MRS. D. Did she go alone ?

PREN. No ; Mrs. Andrews came for her in her carriage.

MRS. D. Who is Mrs. Andrews ?

PREN. A new friend of my wife's, whom she met at a ball a week ago, a charming little woman whom nobody knows anything about.

MRS. D. She owns a carriage ?

PREN. Yes. Ah ! here comes our Amazon.

Enter MRS. PRENDERGAST.

MRS. P. (*gaily*) Good morning, Eleanor; how do, Hubby?'
Here I am safe and sound, no bones broken, not even a hair
turned, as Mrs. Andrews would say.

MRS. D. Two months of this prescription and you will be
restored to perfect health, I hope.

MRS. P. How satirical you are! But just ask Prendie if
I haven't been ailing and low-spirited, and now look at me,
as gay as a butterfly! How I wish it was Thursday.

PREN. Why Thursday? Oh! I forgot Mrs. George
Reynolds' ball.

MRS. D. Are you invited?

PREN. Yes, her brother, Fred Livingstone, has sent us an
invitation.

MRS. P. And what a delightful brother he is. I really
don't know how we should get on without brothers—other
people's, of course. And how splendidly he rides.

MRS. D. Yes, and he has fine horses.

MRS. P. Then he ought to be happy. I adore horses.
Apropos. I am going to the races on Monday with Amabelle.

MRS. D. Amabelle?

MRS. P. Mrs. Andrews.

MRS. D. Already at Christian names!

MRS. P. Oh yes; express trains for me in all things. (*to*
MR. PRENDERGAST) You will accompany me?

PREN. I'm scarcely intimate enough with your friends—
I——

MRS. P. Oh, that's nothing! Such old-fashioned ceremony's
exploded. We share the expenses—don't frown, dear, it
will not be much; so say you'll go; besides, we are never
seen out together; and people hardly know whether I'm
maid, wife, or widow.

PREN. I'll go.

MRS. P. And now excuse me a moment, while I doff my
riding dress.   (*Exit*)

PREN. (*after a short silence, and with some hesitation*) She
is fond of amusement, Eleanor; but then her age——

MRS. D. Exactly.

PREN. And these pleasures are all innocent.

MRS. D. Certainly.

PREN. And I assure you, Eleanor, she does not exceed
our means.

MRS. D. So much the better. Your income, however, is
not more than five hundred a year.

PREN. A little more—say seven; and then I am living
rent free, in my own house, you know, so that——

Mrs. D. I spend double five hundred and you know how we live.

Prex. Well, well, I am like a good Catholic, I stint my-self to decorate the Madonna; and then Cecilia knows how to make a little go a great way, and you have no idea of the wonderful bargains she makes! This is an extraordinary city for lucky chances in the way of purchases, if you know the right way to go about it. It takes a great deal of time to be sure, and your dear child demands all yours, while as to Cecilia——

Mrs. D. As to Cecilia, half her time is taken up with acquiring luxuries, and the other half in exhibiting them. What is there left for you?

Prex. Well, well, I am not exacting.

Mrs. D. But I can be exacting for you—I, who love—I, who owe you happiness, fortune—I, whose whole life has been influenced for good by you, dear guardian.

Prex. Eleanor!

Mrs. D. You have given me the right to regard myself as your daughter, and I take the right to be concerned for the happiness of one who thinks but of others' welfare. Cecilia, from pure giddiness, I am sure, seems to forget what she owes you!

Prex. She owes me nothing. It is I who am the debtor. Without her my existence had been almost a blank, and I owe to her some years of a contentment so perfect that it will be a charm for the rest of my days. And, besides, it is all your fault.

Mrs. D. My fault?

Prex. Yes; for while I was your guardian, time passed swiftly and calmly, and it was only when you were married that I discovered myself, some distance past my "forty years," alone and useless, my life having no farther aim——

Mrs. D. Then I ought to have remained a minor for ever, eh?

Prex. Precisely, but you came of age, married, and—and I met Cecilia. I was in a good position; I was no longer young, it is true, but I was not old, and—and she consented to marry me. I made her my wife, and life recommenced; and do not be uneasy on my account, Eleanor—I am happy.

Mrs. D. Really happy? I find you changed.

Prex. I am getting old.

Mrs. D. No! You work too hard, simply because Cecilia spends more money than she ought, a fact I should like to make her comprehend.

Prex. Pray say nothing; the least cloud between you two would bring a heavy shadow upon me.

Mrs. D. Oh, she will not take it ill; she knows I am her friend. Her head is light, but I think her heart is good. When she learns the labour it costs you to procure her one dress——

Pren. She would go without it, and that I do not wish. If we were nearer in age I should think differently, but as it is, the matter rests in this wise : I have full confidence in her rectitude, and my wife shall be happy if it is in my power to make her so. I do not deceive myself, Eleanor ; friendship and gratitude are the only feelings she *can* experience for me. I will secure as much of these as I may. And that is one reason why I tolerate certain extravagances which clash with my position, and why I beg of you not to speak to her of this frivolity, which, at all events, prevents her from contemplating too minutely the real void in her existence !

Mrs. D. How you love her !

Enter Mrs. Prendergast.

Mrs. P. (*to* Mrs. Duval) Is your dress for Thursday ready ?

Mrs. D. Yes, and has been since the last ba'l I went to.

Pren. There !

Mrs. P. But not here. (*indicating her dress*) Mine will be a perfect chef d' œuvre. Fancy——

Pren. Ah, you are going to talk femininities. Ladies, your most obedient. I have some work to finish.

They salute. Exit Prendergast. Mrs. Duval *seats herself*, L. Mrs. Prendergast, *after a look in the mirror, comes and sits near her.*

Mrs. P. Fancy, my dear Eleanor, a toilette that will make them all mad with envy.

Mrs. D. What is the material of your dress ?

Mrs. P. Oh, the dress is the least part of it.

Mrs. D. You alarm me ! Lace ?

Mrs. P. That is my secret ; wait till Thursday.

Mrs. D. Take care not to be too well dressed for your husband's position.

Mrs. P. Who need know that he is my husband ?

Mrs. D. Enough that he is. You have strange ideas sometimes, Cecilia.

Mrs. P. Well, there, never mind. Bye-the-bye, we count upon you and Alfred—that is, your husband—to dinner on Saturday.

Mrs. D. No, you will have company.

Mrs. P. Yourselves included, ten persons only ; and you shall see the dinner service I have just bought.

Mrs. D. Oh yes, your "great bargain" of last month.

Mrs. P. Bargain, indeed! A complete table service, porcelain, glass, and napkins, all new, by an extraordinary coincidence marked with our cipher!

Mrs. D. What a singular chance.

Mrs. P. And you know what an impossibly low price I paid for it.

Mrs. D. No one like you for these fortunate discoveries.

Mrs. P. I! I was born too late; I should have discovered America, if it had been for sale.

Mrs. D. And, as usual, would have bought it for next to nothing.

Mrs. P. You malicious creature. But really in large cities, you may pick up "bargains" as easily as you pluck wild strawberries in the woods.

Mrs. D. But you will tire yourself out in this chase after bargains.

Mrs. P. No, for I have found what I wanted, my lace.

Mrs. D. Then you have lace?

Mrs. P. Well, yes, I may as well confess, enough English point for six flounces, and the corsage, rescued from the wreck of a certain divinity who——

Mrs. D. How! you do not disdain to pick up the waifs and strays of——

Mrs. P. Oh, what can it matter? Besides, they have scarcely been worn. What have you to say now?

Mrs. D. That they have been too much worn for me.

Mrs. P. You are proud!

Mrs. D. Fastidious rather. I like to feel at home in my garments, completely at home.

Mrs. P. Oh, of course, of course; but I could not resist the temptation; and when this lace was offered to me——

Mrs. D. You spoke of sale.

Mrs. P. Yes, yes; how particular you are. I arranged to examine it first, for in a question of fifty pounds——

Mrs. D. Fifty pounds! Fifty pounds for a quantity of English point like that! You must either be mistaken or deceived.

Mrs. P. Well, never mind. Wait till you see it.

Mrs. D. And the money?

Mrs. P. The money! Now don't scold. Don't say anything to Prendergast, you old-fashioned darling, you!

Mrs. D. Secrets from him?

Mrs. P. (*a little embarrassed*) He is so good, you know, that I am sure he would have found me the money. But, however, I thought—in fact, I had some jewels of my mother's that I had no use for——

Mrs. D. You never spoke of them to me!

Mrs. P. Oh, a lot of last generation rings and things—and —and—I sold them.

Mrs. D. But suppose your husband should ask for them?

Mrs. P. Oh, he has never heard of them.

Mrs. D. Never heard of them!

Mrs. P. It wasn't wrong, was it? You quite frighten me. A lot of stupid stones mounted in the year——

Mrs. D. Never mind the year. They once belonged to your mother?

Mrs. P. Certainly, but as they were no longer in fashion——

Mrs. D. I am afraid, Cecilia, you and I will never understand each other. You admit, of course, that you being dead, your children——

Mrs. P. Oh, nonsense! I have no children.

Mrs. D. Do you desi e none?

Mrs. P. No indeed! No mat rnal slavery for me!

Mrs. D. (*with dignity*) If you thi k so, at least refrain from saying so. (*bell*; Mrs. Prendergast *goes up stage*)

Liv. (*outside*) Do not let me disturb you, Mr. Prendergast.

Mrs. P. Ah! Mr. Fred Livingstone.

Enter LIVINGSTONE.

Liv. (*bows to* Mrs. Prendergast, *and then addresses* Mrs. Duval) Alfred is not with you?

Mrs. D. No, but I have a rendezvous here with him. I begin to fear though—— (*looking at her watch*)

Liv. (*to* Mrs. Prendergast) Mr. Prendergast is in his study. What an indefatigable worker he is. If he had made the world in six days, I would wager he would have taken no rest on the seventh.

Pren. (*entering*) And you would have won, my dear Livingstone. Your sister is very kind to think of us for her party.

Liv. And you are very kind to accept the invitation; we want some solid men to counteract us butterflies.

Pren. Well, why not cease to be a butterfly, and become a quiet humble bee of domesticity——

Mrs. D. With a queen bee to rule your hive.

Liv Now! well, not at present. I live like a traveller, observing, noting, remembering, always cautious, always discreet. I have made the tour of the world like Scarmentado, but I do not intend to finish as he did.

Mrs. P. Scarmentado?

Liv. An unfortunate traveller, Mrs. Prendergast, who imprudently returned home and married.

Mrs. D As we shall see you, some day.

Liv. No, for a thousand reasons; firstly—don't be frigh⸗ tened, I'm not going through the whole thousand—firstly, one always marries to pay something—I have no debts. And, secondly, marriage has become a ruinous speculation, since there set in this deadly and interminable rivalry among wives as to whose bill at the dressmaker's shall be the longest.

Mrs. D. Demand sumptuary laws.

Liv. And the woman would demand my head.

Pren.
Mrs. P. } They would!
Mrs. D.

LIVINGSTONE *has picked up the newspaper, and is reading it; laughs.*

Pren. What are you laughing at?

Liv. (*reading*) "To Cabmen.—Lost, a Gold Lady's Watch." (*all laugh*) Ah, we shall never know why broughams and cabs, at so much an hour, should be dowered with such miscellaneous articles as purses, stockbrokers' memorandum books, embroidered handkerchiefs, photographs, bracelets, bottles of medicine, lawyers' notes, and barristers' briefs, etc., etc.

M·s. D. Grace for the lawyers!

Liv. I speak by the card, madam; for no longer since than yesterday—but perhaps I ought not to continue.

Mrs. P. As if we were listening!

Liv. Well, Mr. Prendergast, no longer since than yester- day evening, I was smoking my way across Piccadilly, when an elegant little brougham turned the corner of Sackville Street, and suddenly the spring broke.

Mrs. P. Sackville Street?

Liv. Ah, you *are* listening, then. I abridge. I will not paint the flight of the two occupants of the brougham, a lady and gentleman.

Mrs. P. Did you recognise them—follow them?

Liv. No, for by the time I reached the spot—I never hurry—they had disappeared, but I distinctly saw the coach- man draw out a brief and other legal documents, and memoranda—I have seen legal documents and memoranda— ahem! which package said coachman will possibly obtain his fare with—possibly more than his fare.

Mrs. D. (*musing*) A brief, and legal documents.

Mrs. P. (*suddenly*) Are you going to the Opera on Friday, Mr. Livingstone?

Liv. The Bouffe, yes. I have a box at your service, ladies.

Mrs. P. Delighted. I love the Opera Bouffe.

Mrs. D. You must excuse me, Mr. Livingstone, after the ball of Thursday I shall be too fatigued. (*rising as if to go*)

Mrs. P. You leave us?

Mrs. D. Yes, Alfred told me not to expect him after four.

Charlotte *opens door and makes a sign to* Mrs. Prendergast.

Mrs. P. Mr. Livingstone, will you see Mrs. Duval home?

Liv You send me away?

Mrs. P. Yes, for to-day I belong to my household duties.

Liv. Good-day, I will call again during the week. (*offers his arm to* Mrs. Duval; *they exit, followed by* Prendergast)

Char. (*enters, and whispers to* Mrs. Prendergast) Madame Angélique is here, ma'am.

Mrs. P. Immediately.

Pren. (*returning*) Well. shall we play truant to-day?

Mrs. P. No, no; I have to work. I have my dress to make.

Pren. As you please, pet, I will go and earn the trimming for it. (*kisses his hand to her; exit to his study;* Mrs. Prendergast *steps softly after him and gently turns the key*)

Mad. (*enter with* Charlotte *from curtained door*) Your most obedient, madame.

Mrs. P. Hush!

Mad. Ah, Mr. Prendergast is there; exactly! Well, here's the lace, a perfect spider's web, and fit for a duchess, washed like new.

Mrs. P. Superb! Look, Charlotte.

Char. Oh! I've never seen its equal.

Mad. I thought you'd be pleased.

Mrs. P. Enchanted!

Mad. And now let us settle the price.

Mrs. P. Fifty pounds, of course.

Mad. Which with the £250 more you owe me makes £300, and all due on Friday.

Mrs. P. Yes, on Friday.

Mad. Ah! if everybody else was as exact. I am glad you are ready, for I shall want the money.

Mrs. P. Only for this.

Mad. For all, ma'am, for all; and on Friday at two o'clock, at the latest.

Mrs. P. Friday! All! Charlotte!

Char. She's a regular vampire!

Mad. I could sell this for ready money, and if I give you the preference——

Mrs. P. I mean the old debt; it is too bad, after I have dealt with you for three years. You surely will not refuse me a little more time for the £250.

MAD. Not a day ; why should I ? Besides there's no need. What is the use of your being young and pretty if you can't wheedle your old husband out of a few hundreds extra ? He won't cry much more over a good molar of £300 than he would over three small teeth of a hundred each. Don't make two bites of a cherry. Try him !

MRS. P. What must be, must ; and I daresay it will come out all right. Friday then at two. You shall have your money somehow. Friday—fortunate I'm not superstitious.

(Exit

MAD. Oh, these poor devils of husbands. Here, Charlotte, there's something for yourself.

CHAR. Thank you for nothing. Madame Angélique, you may keep your money.

MAD. I will keep it, and I'm not at all offended, young woman. (<i>on the threshold</i>) When you are married, come to me for your wreath and veil. (<i>going</i>)

CHAR. Madame Angelic, (<i>aside</i>) Mrs. Angel. (<i>aloud</i>) I say Madame Angelic. (<i>she returns</i>)

MAD. Well ?

CHAR. Parly voo frongsay ? (<i>laughs heartily as</i> MADAME ANGELIQUE <i>flounces out</i>)

CURTAIN.

ACT II.

SCENE. —DUVAL'S <i>house.</i>   <i>Library.</i>   <i>Writing-desk, etc.</i>
    LIVINGSTONE <i>and</i> DUVAL <i>discovered.</i>

DUV. There's my I.O.U.

LIV. For a few miserable pounds I have lent you. Pooh ! (<i>tearing up paper</i>) Between friends such commercial superstitions are scarcely the thing. You can repay me at your own sweet will.

DUV. A thousand thanks.

LIV. A hundred will suffice. Let's change the conversation. I have given my landlady notice, Alfred.

DUV. Going to change your apartments !

LIV. Refreshing innocent ! the landlady of my heart, the proprietress of my soul. My roving eyes are now fixed elsewhere.

DUV. Might one ask upon what fortunate mortal you have fixed them ?

LIV. One might ask—yes.

Duv. (*with hesitation*) Can it possibly be Mrs. Prendergast?

Liv. If anyone asks *you* such a question, say you don't know.

Duv. And I say to you that I have every right to ask such a question, for I will allow no one to bring trouble into a household the disturbance of whose repose would affect my own.

Liv. Keep calm, Alfred ; you know me little if you suppose I could do anything to interfere with the serenity of Prendergast, who is planted in our century like an image of virtue on a tombstone. Only if your repose depends upon the behaviour of the saintly Cecilia, the partner of his respectable bosom, you may, with justice, be somewhat uneasy.

Duv. Livingstone, I beg you will refrain—How can you possibly ? Such imputations as these should not be advanced without proofs or——

Liv. Proofs ! Ho ! ho ! plentiful as blackberries ! Her luxury is a confirmation, her wardrobe an endorsement, and one single robe of the many she displays would suffice to hang her, if hanging were the appointed punishment for such matrimonial fallings away. In short, sweet Mistress Cecilia belongs to that class of ambitious feminines who, like claret, would be port if they could, and who not being rich by nature, become so by art.

Duv. But this apparent luxury is easily explained ; a good housewife saves sufficient from the household expenses allowance——

Liv. Up to a certain point I grant you, and as long as the claret in question is a sound, pure wine, the husband pays fifty per cent. increase on his marketings ; but the moment our claret—we'll keep up the metaphor—becomes adulterated and descends from its high estate, the case is reversed and his purchases actually cost him half or a quarter of their value, so that our ambitious claret who commences by robbing the household, finishes by enriching it.

Duv. You seem deeply versed in the matter.

Liv. Experience, observation ; our classes we go through at college, our humanities we study in the world, and I flatter myself I know something of it. Delightful victories are won : but victory is often costly ! "Delightful !" Yes, the idea of these conquests is very fascinating. Like the apples of the Dead Sea, they are rosy and captivating to the view, but like those same apples, they contain nothing but ashes. Forbidden fruit, Alfred, better leave it on the tree, better leave it on the tree.

Duv. You are right ; you are right. (*stiffly*) But still I cannot, will not credit such unfounded assertions, made, too, on such slight grounds, and I will never admit that Mrs. Prendergast may be seriously accused of conduct impossible without the connivance of her husband, a thing not to be thought of for a moment.

LIV. Prendergast's connivance! That's too good! He has no more suspicion of anything wrong than I have of anything right. He never imagines a clandestine sovereign enters his premises. Well, I will bet a trifle that our sweet young friend, Mrs. Prendergast, one year with another, introduces into the household four or five hundred of the little hypocrites.

DUV. (angrily) This persistence is in excessively bad taste, Mr. Livingstone!

LIV. So! you are becoming bitter. Let us drop the subject then; any way, I am totally disinterested!

DUV. And I. Do you suppose I am defending anything but the cause of truth?

LIV. The cause of truth—humph! you defend it with a good deal of fire.

DUV. How absurd you are. Can you expect me to believe——

LIV. Ah! you are returning to the subject.

DUV. Well, yes, and from your vast fund of information on the matter, I would ask your instruction on one point. The lover may be possible——

LIV. Oh, you grant that?

DUV. But how in the name of chicanery, a woman can spend all this extra money on the house without the husband's knowledge, passes my comprehension.

LIV. I will tell you a fable. A.B. has a wife. Said wife by dint of much coaxing and wheedling extracts from A.B. a necklace of false diamonds, value, say £40. Five years later Mrs. A.B. dies. After the customary mourning has been gone through, A.B. thinks he may as well sell his necklace, takes it to a jeweller, who, after a careful examination, offers him £500! difference—four hundred and sixty. A.B. is stupified, but takes the goods the Gods provide him, the real meaning of the matter being easily explained by experts. And so wags the world. There is a Love Exchange as well as a commercial one, and stocks are sold and resold continually. Pride, vanity, luxury, lace, bijouterie, and vertu—not virtue—there we are! and that explains the whole matter.

DUV. But it by no means explains the application of your worldly theories to an intimate friend of my wife's, whom, by that title alone, you ought to respect.

LIV. (looking at him meaningly) Friend Alfred, I actually and seriously think that I respect her more than you do!

Duv. What do you mean?

Liv. I mean that you defend her like an accomplice.

Duv. An accomplice—I! You are mad!

Liv. Not so mad as you think. Let us talk plainly. Your position in life is excellent, this house belongs to your wife, you do not live extravagantly, and yet you have to borrow—no reproach intended—deduction from these premises, you spend money secretly.

Duv. (*embarrassed*) I have made some disastrous speculation. There—keep my secret!

Liv. (*drily*) Your confidence honours me! (*aside*) Humbug! (*aloud*) I imagined there might be some little *liaison*, perhaps some——

Duv. How? Do you suppose I, a married man, would deliberately——

Liv. Oh, deliberation has nothing to do with it. These charming little partnerships are brought about without the least premeditation. Guileless little presents are rained down; it goes sweetly on, beautifully; and then, one day, comes a deficit in the household budget, and the faithful shepherd offers his purse. One loves or one does not love. She loves and she accepts.

Duv. (*hanging his head down*) It is true; but as soon as he discovers it, he——

Liv. Ah! it seems I have lifted the scales from your eyes. Well, I ask you no questions. Confidence, entire and reciprocal, is the device of friendship; and having given you my mind, I will leave you. Good morning, Mr. Alfred Duval, verdant citizen of the metropolis and possible shepherd.

(*Exit*)

Enter Mrs. Duval.

Duv. Why should he come and lay his finger on my wound? why—Eleanor! I feel a pang at my heart every time I behold her.

Mrs. D. Mr. Livingstone is gone at last. What had he got to say of such importance?

Duv. Oh, he was merely passing, and stepped in to shake hands with me.

Mrs. D. He took his time.

Duv. Does the chatterer ever finish?

Mrs. D. He has wit, for all his chattering.

Duv. Unfortunately! For wit, with a tongue like his, is as dangerous as a loaded pistol in the hands of a child. He has lost me my morning. Do we go to the theatre on Saturday?

Mrs. D. I have already refused, but that need not hinder you from going.

Duv. Without you!

Mrs. D. Cecilia will be there, and Mr. Prendergast; and if the piece should not please you——

Duv. Scylla and Charybdis—delightful choice between the conversation of Cecilia and that patriarchal pedagogue, her husband.

Mrs. D. Alfred, you are lately rather hard towards my dear guardian. Try and change your manner, as it appears to me your example has some effect in increasing the unceremonious treatment his wife has recently adopted towards him.

Duv. Her behaviour has nothing to do with me, and, apropos, I do not understand why for some time past you have made me responsible for her fantasies.

Mrs. D. I am wrong, perhaps, but I think so much of the happiness of that worthy man, to whom we owe our fortune, that my uneasiness is greater than his own. He has none, he is so good.

Duv. Oh, an angel, of course.

Mrs. D. (after a short pause, as if from indignation) A heart simple and tender, an upright mind, and an honesty beyond proof, has this patriarchal pedagogue, as it pleases you to call him. (rising and going near him) And this man helped you in your first efforts to establish yourself, was a second father to me, married me to you whom I loved, and whom, but for him, I might never have married. The day I became his ward I was almost poor; when he resigned his charge I was almost rich; while he has no more than he had twenty years ago, for his own interests are always forgotten in those of others. If there be anything ridiculous in this man, his noble qualities hide it, at least from my eyes!

Duv. Why recall obligations which——

Mrs. D. Be assured he does not remember them.

Duv. Oh, I do not forget them, but—but—it is getting late, I ought to be at chambers. Have you anything to ask me?

Mrs. D. (with some hesitation) The month ends to-morrow —the servants' wages——

Duv. You have no money?

Mrs. D. None.

Duv. And I am in the same condition, I have no money.

Mrs. D. Get some! we women do not enter into details in this matter.

Duv. Our boy costs me a great deal.

Mrs. D. From funds invested for him.

Duv. (giving money from his desk) Is that enough?

Mrs. D. Too much.

Duv. (*with tenderness*) Take it nevertheless, you must not be inconvenienced for want of money; but be economical, dear Eleanor.

Mrs. D. I am ; this year's expenses so far have been less than last. (Duval *is searching all through his desk*)

Duv. Where in the name of Heaven is that brief, "Luttrell and Luttrell."

Mrs. D. A brief !

Duv. Have you seen it ?

Mrs. D. No, I never come here when you are away.

Duv. I wish the servants would leave my desk alone. I have forbidden them a hundred times to "arrange" it, but it seems I am not to be obeyed.

Mrs. D. I will call John, perhaps he has seen it. (*rising*)

Duv. (*as if suddenly remembering*) No, never mind, I must have left it at chambers : don't trouble ! besides, I have no time to wait now.

Mrs. D. Have you looked thoroughly ?

Duv. Yes ! yes ! it is not here. Good-bye, shall be back soon !   (*Exit hurriedly*)

> Mrs. Duval *searches desk and room with a sort of fury for a few minutes, and finally as she sinks, full of agitation, on a lounge,* Prendergast *enters.*

Pren. It is I, my dear child ; I have given myself a holiday to-day, and am going to take you to the flower-show. I have sent a messsage to Cecilia to join us here. But what were you looking for in such excitement ?

Mrs. D. (*who has continued her search*) Nothing. (*aside*) That brief must be here ! It is impossible that—Oh, I am mad to think !

Pren. What is it ? what are you looking for ?

Mrs. D. (*shewing bank notes*) One of these notes I thought I had lost.

Pren. (*smiling*) And you have them in your hand all the while. Master Alfred is generous. 'Tis easy enough to see he is doing well.

Mrs. D. He does not acknowledge it.

Pren. He must have gained seven or eight hundred this year already.

Mrs. D. Eight hundred pounds !

Pren. At the least.

Mrs. D. I should never have believed it.

Pren. Why not?

Mrs. D. He does not gamble ; his tastes are simple as my own, and yet I cannot express to you the embarrassment I feel when I have to ask him for money.

PREN. Is it possible he speculates?

MRS. D. No. I feel sure!

PREN. I will see him, and catechise him sharply, I promise you, and you shall soon have an explanation of the mystery.

MRS. D. Do! do! I beg of you; and let him tell me, even if it be the loss of our entire fortune. I shall count myself still rich if he remains to me.

PREN. With what emotion you say that. Always the same, Eleanor, always the same.

Enter JOHN *with letter.*

MRS. D. What is it?

JOHN. An account, madam, for Mr. Duval.

MRS. D. Did you say he was out?

JOHN. I did, madam, but the person has been several times, and——

PREN. Pay it from the money you have, Eleanor; it does not look well for creditors to come so often in vain.

MRS. D. Give me the account. (*opens it and reads, while* PRENDERGAST *is occupied with the newspaper*) A bonnet-maker's bill! (*reads items for an ultra-fashionable and expensive bonnet. The same as worn by* MRS. PRENDERGAST) Five pounds! *to* JOHN) There must be some mistake!

JOHN. No, madam. I heard master tell the person to call again.

MRS. D. (*thunderstruck*) Ah! (*gives bill to* JOHN) Pay it, five pounds. (*Exit* JOHN)

PREN. Five pounds!

MRS. D. (*with intensity*) For a bonnet!

PREN. A bonnet!

MRS. D. (*aside*) My heart did not deceive me!

PREN. For you?

MRS. D. For me! My bonnets cost a fifth of that sum, and I cheapen my dresses like a miser, saving every possible shilling, while my husband squanders his son's fortune, and uses that son's name to blind me, and to serve as a screen for his profligacy!

PREN. Calm yourself, Eleanor.

MRS. D. You wondered what I was looking for with such eagerness when you came in. 'Twas that brief, the brief left in a carriage, the day before yesterday. You remember? he left it.

PREN. He? Alfred!

MRS. D. If I were not sure already, this (*shewing account*) is proof en ough.

PREN. Impossible! Alfred is devoted to his profession, and is that the only brief in this great city?

MRS. D. For me, yes ! and this account, this account ! I understand now why he is so short of money. I understand now why he so suddenly discontinued his search for the brief. He knew too well where he had left it. Oh, I do not suspect him for the first time to-day. Idiot that I have been to economise, that he might scatter my savings in such directions!

PREN. My child, be calm, reflect.

MRS. D. I have reflected. When he returns here he will find me gone, and she who has chased me from his heart may take my place in his house.

PREN. But your son?

MRS. D. Goes with me. Will he dare dispute my right to him ?

PREN. But hear.

MRS. D. I will hear nothing ! the separation is accomplished ! at no price will I submit to this shameful complicity.

PREN. But think of the scandal—the future destroyed; Alfred's career——

MRS. D. Of vice ! and this woman must have such bonnets as this ! Read that ! (*gives him account*)

PREN. Some one is coming. Alfred, perhaps.

MRS. D. If it be, read it aloud.

Enter MRS. PRENDERGAST *with the bonnet precisely as described in the account.*

MRS. P. Here I am ! are we all ready? Good morning, Eleanor. What, not dressed yet? Do, for goodness' sake, get ready.

MRS. D. (*her eyes on the ground, and absently*) Yes, yes.

MRS. P. We shall get there just as everybody's going away. (*goes to glass and arranges her head-dress*)

MRS. D. Go without me. I am not well. I have told your husband. (*languidly raises her eyes, and seems turned to stone as she sees* MRS. PRENDERGAST'S *bonnet*) The very bonnet ! (*then as she turns and sees* PRENDERGAST *about to read the account she utters a cry, and rushes towards him, tears the bill from his hand, and hoarsely says, aside*) He must not know ! (*aloud*) Not a word to Alfred ! to any one. I must reflect.

MRS. P. What is the matter, Eleanor dear?

PREN. Do not question her, Cecilia, she is not well this morning—low spirits. Try and come with us, Eleanor, the fresh air will do you good.

MRS. P., (*approaching; as she does so,* MRS. DUVAL *recoils toward* PRENDERGAST) And you are so fond of flowers ! Do come !

MRS. D. I prefer—to remain—at home!

PREN. Come, come, a little courage!

MRS. D. Courage! I have more than you think!

MRS. P. Are you looking at my new bonnet?

MRS. D. (*quickly*) No! no!

MRS. P. Come, make an effort, Eleanor.

MRS. D. No, I will stay here. (*aside to* PRENDERGAST)
Take her away! I would be alone! and remember, not a
word!

PREN. I promise. (*to* MRS. PRENDERGAST) Come, Cecilia
we are driven away.

MRS. P. Good-bye, Eleanor; take care of yourself. Good-
bye. (*she bends and offers her face to* MRS. DUVAL *to be kissed;*
MRS. DUVAL, *under the looks of* PRENDERGAST, *slightly passes
her lips against* MRS. PRENDERGAST'S *forehead, visibly shudder-
ing as she does so*)

PREN. Come, let us be off. (*exeunt;* PRENDERGAST
returning a moment after)

PREN. I forgot my gloves. Now don't make yourself
ill. Be reasonable. Scold him! scold him well! but no
scandal.

MRS. D. Fear nothing! fear nothing!

PREN. And should there be anything new, write to me
at once.

MRS. D. Yes, yes, thanks! (*Exit* PRENDERGAST. *She
reads the account again*) Am I ready now? She! Cecilia!
she, *indeed!* Blind, blind, blind, blind that I was! Heaven
be praised, her husband knows nothing, suspects nothing;
nor shall he. I will be the only sufferer. Heaven help me!
Heaven help me! (*sinks sobbing on a fauteuil*)

CURTAIN.

ACT III.

SCENE.—*An elegant suite of apartments at* MRS. GEORGE
REYNOLDS'. *Dancers and music, etc.* MRS. PRENDERGAST
and LIVINGSTONE *on lounge.* MRS. PRENDERGAST *finishing
an ice.*

MRS. P. Do you know you are very compromising?

LIV. Is it my fault that you are adorable, and that I adore
you? logical cause and effect, you see.

MRS. P. Will you be quiet, or at least speak low?

LIV. Whispers will suit me perfectly. (*they appear to talk*)

1ST GUEST. Isn't she delicious?

2ND GUEST. A delicious woman and a delicious toilette! looks like a duchess.

3RD GUEST. (*just entering*) A duchess! where?

2ND GUEST. There before you.

3RD GUEST. That a duchess! why it's only the wife of old Prendergast, the lawyer.

1ST GUEST. He must be as rich as old.

3RD GUEST. Rich! about enough to make both ends meet.

1ST GUEST. Where does such a dress as that come from then?

3RD GUEST. And echo answers where!

2ND GUEST. I should like a galop with her.

3RD GUEST. I dare say you would, but her card is full, and the next number, a waltz, is mine. (*advances to* MRS. PREN-DERGAST) Madame, I have the pleasure to claim your hand for this waltz

MRS. P. (*consulting her card, and with an air of vexation*) You are right, sir. Excuse me, Mr. Livingstone.

(*Exit with partner ; two others follow*)

Enter MRS. REYNOLDS.

REY. Frederic, who is this gorgeous beauty you brought here to-night? she is making quite a commotion among my guests.

LIV. A commotion!

REY. Yes. I hear remarks, some not over agreeable, on all sides about her. Is she qu te comme il faut?

LIV. Shoul l I have presented her to you had it been otherwise? She goes into all society.

REY. Like people who belong to none! What is her husband?

LIV. A solicitor.

REY. A solicitor's wife, and toilette like that? and is it to conciliate him that you are so specially attentive to her?

LIV. Oh, you women! if a man is a little polite to one of your sex, not over plain ——

REY. Say no more, but expect not another blank ticket of invitation from me.

LIV. Why, what has she done?

REY. Her presence embarrasses me, for her dress, lace, and ornaments by no means correspond with her husband's position, and in short——

LIV. In short, what feminine speciality do you desire for your parties?

Enter MR. *and* MRS. DUVAL.

REY. Here is my model!

Liv. Couldn't have happened better; ask your model about Mrs. Prendergast.

Rey. (*advancing cordially to* Mrs. Duval) How late you are, my dear Mrs. Duval.

Mrs. D. We are indeed late, but you will excuse us, I am sure.

Liv. (*to* Duval) Good evening, my virtuous friend.

Duv. Good evening.

Rey. (*to* Mrs. Duval) Frederic was just telling me that you are acquainted with Mrs. Prendergast.

Mrs. D. Yes, I know her *well*; her husband has been more than a father to me, and I venerate and love him.

Rey. His wife is very pretty, but she seems to me rather flighty ; slightly prononcée.

Mrs. D. A spoilt child, nothing more.

Rey. She has attracted great attention here to night ; and if one may judge by her dress, her husband must be the most generous of men.

Mrs. D. He loves her devotedly.

Rey. She must be in the ball-room now; shall we go there ?

Mrs. D. If you wish.

Rey. Where she obtained such marvellous flowers in the month of December is past my knowledge of such matters ; there was a perfect buzz of admiration.

Mrs. D. He is ruining himself for her. (*they leave the room talking*)

Liv. Have a glass of champagne, Alfred ?

Duv. Thank you, nothing.

Liv. What's the matter ? anyone would think you had come to a funeral instead of a ball, with that solemn face.

Duv. If you must know, I am in a state of the greatest anxiety.

Liv. As to what?

Duv. I want £300.

Liv. I see—a new anxiety on an old subject.

Duv. Could you possibly lend me the amount for a week?

Liv. If I had it, yes ; but I have not.

Duv. It is a debt of honour.

Liv. In that case I must try to help you. A gambling debt ?

Duv. Oblige me doubly by not questioning me.

Liv. Delightful philosophy ! Livingstone, my dear friend, snatch me out of the fire, but don't ask me how I fell in.

Duv. I cannot possibly tell you.

Liv. You need not. I can picture the whole scene. You visit your shepherdess ; she is leaning sadly on her crook, in tears ; you imprudently ask her what is the particular afflic-

tion ; she sobbingly refuses to tell you.   In such a case **I**
pursue the subject no further, but there are shepherds vernal
enough to insist ; well, *you* insist until the shepherdess, with
two large tears—pearls to judge by their cost—rolling down
her peachy cheeks, confesses all—a debt, a simple debt ;
and the shepherd, tenderly drying her eyes, takes the responsibility upon his devoted shoulders, and hence Alfred Duval
comes to his friend, Fred Livingstone, for £300.

Duv. I swear to you that——

Liv. Confidence entire, or——

Duv. Well, suppose a creditor does threaten to ruin by
exposure a woman, I—I am doing my duty, and you as a
man of the world, what have you to say to that ?

Liv. What have I to say ? simply that you have a wife
and a child, and that I will not further assist you in such
procedures.   But don't trouble yourself ; your shepherdess
will get out of the scrape without you.

Duv. No ! besides, my honour is pledged. I must raise
the money, and then I break the connection for ever.

Liv. Ah !

Duv. Yes ; the opportunity is too good to lose ; you will
help me, won't you ? (Livingstone *tapping his pocket and
shrugging his shoulders, exits. Duval follows*) But, Livingstone—Fred !   (*Exit*)

Enter from opposite door, Mr. Gosling *and* Amanda.

Gos. It won't do, Mandie, it *won't* do ; the man's a hass,
a hass, Mandie !

Am. If you must call Mr. Greenway an ass, papa, at least,
do so without the superfluous H.

Gos. Shan't do nothin' of the kind.   He sounds more a
hass *with* the H.   He's a regular noosance.

Am. Nui—Papa !

Gos. New papa ! *what* do you mean ?

Am. Not new papa—nuisance ! You said *noo*-sance !

Gos. And noosance he is !   A man as can only say " yes "
and " no," and as always, always, *always* agrees with you.
It reg'larly bowls me over !   What his father went and died
in Hindia for, and left him and his five hundred a year for me
to take care of, I can't think ! *I* never die in Hindia, and leave
noosances about like that !   He ain't got no more sense than
a chicken, Miss Gosling, and I should like to wring his neck
accordin' !

Am. My dear papa ! I may not be able to shield poor Mr.
Greenway from your attacks, but I must beg of you to spare
me all allusions to your former low occupation ! A poulterer !

Gos. Low as it was, Miss Gosling, it rais'd you !

AM. I can't help that, papa, but *you* can help talking about it ! And pray don't call me "Gosling" (*with contempt*) when you can possibly avoid it !

Gos. Why, you are a "gosling" ain't you? And as to poultering being " low," let me tell you as the Goslings have had the tiptoppest connections. Why your grandfather poultered George IV. ! There ! And then as to not calling you "Gosling," I look upon that name as a good homen ! It is a sort of a trade mark, and fits in A 1—" Gosling and Co., Poulterers."

AM. But, papa dear, you are not in the trade now, not in trade at all. Goodness be praised ! But here's Mr. Greenway coming, do change the conversation.

Enter GREENWAY.

Gos. All right. It's the unjustest, riduculousest style o' doin' things as ever I met. Why should he come to me to borrow fifty pounds ? *I* never want to borrow fifty pounds, and lost it at cards. Why didn't he go to them as does borrow fifty pounds, and as does lose money at cards, that's what I want to know ?

AM. As *do* lose, as *do*, papa, not as does. Oh, what a thing it is to have a grammarless papa ! Young Mr. Greenway ?

GREEN. Yes, Miss Amanda.

Gos. Don't you be always a-flinging grammar in your parent's face, Miss Gosling. I made my money withou t grammar, I've kep you in elegance and giv' you a Belgravian education without grammar, and when I die, I can leave you enough to live upon, without grammar—there ! *What* do *you* say, young Mr. Greenway ?

GREEN. Yes, Mr. Gosling.

Gos. And you are the first of the Goslings as ever rode in a carriage, Miss Amanda, and proud enough you are o' them horses, as don't know no more o' grammer than I do. And neither them nor me wants to know, Miss Amanda Gosling.

AM. Gosling ! oh, the hideous name, isn't it, young Mr. Greenway ?

GREEN. Yes, Miss Gosling.

AM. Now *he's* "Gos-ling." Well, papa, never mind the grammar now ; but 1 really think you might have lent Mr. Watson the money ; he's a very genteel person.

Gos. Genteel ! pooh ! bosh ! fiddle ! nonsense ! *I* ain't genteel, thank God ! Then what's he come to me for? why don't he go to them as is genteel ?—" let birds of a feather flock together," eh, young Mr. Greenway ?

GREEN. Yes, Mr. Gosling.

AM. Really, papa, I wish you would make no allusions to your former low trade now we are retired. Why should you add to the pangs others inflict on my too sensitive soul?

Gos. What pangs? What are you driving at now?

AM. Why, did you not hear the pointed manner in which that bare-necked old woman in the ball-room asked me if I had read "Foul Play." You did, young Mr. Greenway?

GREEN. Yes, Miss Amanda.

Gos. Think she meant poultry, eh? Well, warn't half a bad joke either—a sharp old girl, Mr. Greenway?

GREEN. Yes, Mr. Gosling.

AM. Oh, papa, how your susceptibilities are blunted!

Gos. Pooh! never had none; howsomever the old girl's no right to begin o'me. I never said nothin' to her. Egad, she's like a old goose herself, with her long scraggy neck! and I'll bet I never sold a tougher.

AM. Oh, papa, do try to catch the tone of society!

Gos. I ain't agoin' to try, Mandie; society never tried to catch *my* tone, and if it wasn't for you I shouldn't never go into society, and that's as sure as eggs is eggs, ain't it, young Greenway?

GREEN. Yes, Mr. Gosling.

AM. "Eggs is eggs!" why, papa, you might as well go back to the old stall in the market at once.

Gos. And nothin' would please me better. I was at home there, and in society I'm as much out of place as an old hen on a tight rope; ain't I, young Greenway?

GREEN. Yes, Mr. Gosling.

AM. Oh, this is too much for my suffering soul. Young Mr. Greenway, I believe I am your partner for the next dance, let us go to the ball-room again.

GREEN. Yes, Miss Amanda.   (*Exeunt*)

Gos. And I'll go below and get a quiet glass of grog. Job Gosling knows what he wants, and the sooner society'll cut him, and folks 'll leave off a asking him for what they ain't got no right to, and Amanda'll shut up on the grammar, the sooner Job Gosling 'll be happy.   (*Exit*)

Enter MRS. DUVAL *in great agitation.*

MRS. D. I can scarcely breathe, I am suffocating with emotion. I see no one, nothing but her in the ball-room. She dared to come and sit near me—*me!* I conquered myself, I spoke to her, and it was *I* who lowered my eyes before *her* gaze. I dared not meet her look, for I felt that my eyes would betray me, and, like vengeful lightning, strike her guilty heart. Oh, heavens! (*enter* PRENDERGAST) Ah, it is you; you are pale, perplexed——

PREN. It is late. I am a little tired. I wished to leave some time since, but Cecilia——

MRS. D. Cannot leave the dance—she has made quite a sensation to-night.

PREN. Yes, yes, too much, too much.

MRS. D. Not for a young and handsome woman, for this success in society is the breath of her life.

PREN. (*after a short pause*) Eleanor, what are your household expenses per annum?

MRS. D. What a singular question to ask at a ball.

PREN. But still if I wish to know.

MRS. D. Well, something like a thousand.

PREN. And you live more quietly than we do.

MRS. D. Why do you ask?

PREN. Nothing—an idea. Tell me, do you know those two old ladies seated near the bay window in the ball-room?

MRS. D. Mrs. Rivers and Lady Granger. I know them well, and excellent women they are.

PREN. I think they are evil-tongued.

MRS. D. They!—indulgence itself!

PREN. Ah!

MRS. D. There is something wrong, dear guardian. Come, make me your confidante.

PREN. (*much moved*) I was standing near those ladies—who do not know me—a short time ago; they were looking at Cecilia dancing, and one said to the other, "There is a woman who gives occasion for much talk about her." "That is true," was the reply; "and people do say that it is not her husband she is ruining."

MRS. D. (*with a forced smile*) And is that all your trouble? Don't annoy yourself over a little feminine gossip; when women once begin to scandalise one of their sex, they seldom know when to stop.

PREN. And yet these two, you said,' were "indulgence itself."

MRS. D. Well, you see I have calumniated them.

PREN. What made it more grave was the fact that they spoke by hearsay. Is it already so public?

MRS. D. I have never heard a word implying what you hint at.

PREN. It is scarcely likely, dear Eleanor, they would have made you the depository of such scandal.

MRS. D. Why, do you think of it then?

PREN. Think! if it were true, it would kill me!

MRS. D. You insult your wife by harbouring the thought for a moment! the supposition is monstrous!

PREN. It is! it is! But yet, why do they speak of it,

why do those two ladies—excellent women both, as you say
—why do they repeat such tales? Are appearances against
her? does she dress too well?

MRS. D. My dear friend, everyone is not in the secret of
her economies, her lucky chances, her bargains; and that is
just the danger of such apparent good fortune, and good
management; it looks as if she spent too much on her toilette;
and as people know you are not rich they try and explain
the elegance of your wife, and malignantly give the reason
you have heard.

PREN. (*bowing his head between his hands, and in an
agitated voice*) I ask myself at last, if it be possible for a
woman to do so much with so little money.

MRS. D. You did not doubt it the other day.

PREN. What does a man like me know of the cost of a
woman's dress? but you—you, one of her own sex, seemed
to doubt it as little as I; and yet now I remember your
manner was constrained.

MRS. D. That was because I feared it would be misunder-
stood, and some day commented upon. Now are you re-
assured?

PREN. (*looking her in the eyes*) If you answer for her, yes.

MRS. D. I answer for her.

PREN. There is yet more. Can you guess what they
added, your two friends? They both agreed that you seemed
to avoid her.

MRS. D. ((*rising*) I! Come with me into the ball-room,
and you and they shall see.

PREN. My own dear child, now, indeed, I am convinced.

(*Exeunt*)

Re-enter GOSLING, AMANDA, *and* GREENWAY.

GOS. That infernal two-horse machine has turned up at
last. What did I want with a carriage, damn the machine!

GREEN. Da-amn the ma——

AM. Young Mr. Greenway, were *you* going to swear?

GREEN. No, Miss Amanda; not—on—purpose.

AM. Papa! if you say that awful word again, I'll faint in
young Mr. Greenway's arms immediately.

GREEN. Yes, Miss Amanda.

GOS. Ain't it grammatic? Any way, it's enough to make
any man break out. Twenty minutes I've bin a pantin', and
a blowin', and a howlin' up the street and round after that
machine, and the hull neighbourhood been a ringin' with
Gosling!

AM. I heard it but too plainly. Oh, the shock! The
atmosphere was full of Goslings! Oh!

Gos. And then the injustness of it. I never kep' nobody a waitin' for his carriage. I never was behind time, and punctualness and Gosling was always anonymous terms when I was in busi——

Am. Papa! be quiet on the spot, I entreat, and let us go home.

Gos. Just what I want, and have wanted ever since I come. Come, young Greenway, we'll drop you as we go—not as ever I asked anybody to drop me; though I suppose you would drop me if you could, young Mr. Greenway?

Green. Yes, Mr. Gosling.

Am. Papa, *will* you come? Young Mr. Greenway, your arm, if you please.

Green. Yes, Miss Amanda..

Am. Oh, that I ever brought papa! Oh, that I ever persuaded Mrs. Reynolds to invite you! I can never look society or Mrs. Reynolds in the face again. (*Exit*)

Gos. (*snaps his fingers*) That much for society! (*Exit*)

Enter Duval *and* Mrs. Prendergast, *in eager conversation.*

Mrs. P. You have not got the money?

Duv. No! nor even a part of it. I have been all over the City to-day, everywhere, and met with nothing but refusals.

Mrs. P. You told me that, if all failed, Mr. Livingstone would lend you the amount.

Duv. He refused to-night, in this very room, and while I lost all I had in the card-room, he won the very amount—£300.

Mrs. P. Then why didn't you ask him again?

Duv. I could not.

Mrs. P. What is to be done?

Duv. I cannot even guess.

Mrs. P. I shall be ruined!

Duv. What can I do? I——

Mrs. P. Hush! here is your wife. (*Enter* Mrs. Duval; *her eyes flash as she sees them together*)

Mrs. D. Alfred, let us go home.

Duv. With pleasure, Eleanor. I will go and see if the carriage is ready. (*Exit*; Mrs. Prendergast *is about returning to the ball-room*)

Mrs. D. Stay! one word, Mrs. Prendergast. Your husband is disquieted, certain rumours have come to his ears to-night. Be careful lest you awaken him from his slumber!

Mrs. P. "Awaken him!"

Mrs. D. I mean what I say. I have averted his suspicions for the time being, for the matter concerns not only his peace of mind. but his life!

Mrs. P. My dear Eleanor, you are speaking in riddles!

Mrs. D. Read them by the light of your own conscience, and profit by my warning.

Mrs. P. (*with an attempt at dignity*) Madame, I fail to see by what right you address me in this extraordinary language! you are exceedingly quick in supposing evil.

Mrs. D. So much the better for you if I am deceiving myself in such supposition!

Mrs. P. 'Tis only you Puritans who make such astonishing discoveries.

Mrs. D. Puritan!

Mrs. P. I suppose you are hinting at Mr. Livingstone! There's no danger, believe me; there is nothing serious about his gallantries, at least as far as I am concerned. I leave the field open to you!

Mrs. D. (*overcome with sudden and uncontrollable indignation at this taunt, draws her figure up to its full height, and looking at* Mrs. Prendergast *with the most overwhelming contempt and anger*) Woman! you have stolen from me my husband! I know everything!

Mrs. P. It—is—false! (*her head droops*)

Mrs. D. It is not false! the very dress you wear to-night is paid for by me! by me! For your bonnet of yesterday I have the receipt! It is *not* false! Never cross my threshold again! Never let me hear your voice, or see your face more! It is NOT false! Invent what pretext you will for the breaking up of our friendship! Friendship! Heaven forgive you—but never darken my doors again! This is all I exact, but this I do exact! Do you hear? Your husband comes! (*looks*) act again!

(*Exit as* Prendergast *enters and gives his arm to* Mrs. Prendergast. *They salute Hostess and other Guests*)

CURTAIN.

ACT IV.

Scene.—*Same as Act I. Laces, ornaments, etc., scattered on table. Boxes on floor. Jewel case on mantel.* Mrs. Prendergast *and* Charlotte *discovered.*

Mrs. P. One o'clock, and Madame Angélique will be here at two.

Char. Yes, ma'am, and not a minute later, trust her for that!

Mrs. P. Are the jewels there?

Char. All in the box, ma'am.

Mrs. P. What do you think they will lend us on them?

Char. Oh, the regular thing, ma'am, a third part of what they are worth!

Mrs. P. It won't be enough! What else can we send? Ah, my watch and chain, and these bracelets. (*puts them in box*)

Char. That's it, ma'am, and if it isn't enough send some of the plate.

Mrs. P. I thought of that, but perhaps Mr. Prendergast might miss it.

Char. Yes, he might, for there's company to-morrow to dinner.

Mrs. P. I will be ill.

Char. I *am* ill. I'll go and get the plate, ma'am. (*Exit*)

Mrs. P. What pillage! What a day! What an exposure if I do not raise the money!—I must write to him.

Char. (*enter with plate basket*) There, ma'am! Oh, my nerves! This ought to be considered in my wages.

Mrs. P. Pack them up. It was a good idea of yours to pawn them; and then perhaps Madame will take some of the things back.

Char. Excuse me, ma'am, but p'raps she won't. (*ring is heard*)

Mrs. P. Oh, if that should be Mr. Prendergast.

Char. No, ma'am, he is in the City safe enough.

Mrs. P. But he sometimes comes in during the day, and his manner was very unusual and peculiar this morning.

Char. Any way, ma'am, he's got the key.

Mrs. P. That's true. Go and open the door, and say I am not at home. (*exit* Charlotte; Mrs. Prendergast *writes*) "Your wife knows all! Adieu!—Cecilia." (*folding and directing*) There, he is warned and dismissed in the same breath. How tragic Eleanor was last night.

Re-enter Charlotte.

Char. Mr. Livingstone, ma'am.

Mrs. P. I told you I was not at home.

Char. He would come in, ma'am; says he wants to see you particular.

Mrs. P. Let him come in, then; and post this letter.

Charlotte *brings in* Livingstone, *and exit.*

Liv. I am as indiscreet as Aurora herself, madame; but I saw that the blinds of your room were drawn; I concluded that you had dawned on the world, and I wished to lay this opera box at the feet of my goddess.

MRS. P. One would think it May instead of December, to hear such glowing language. As to your box I do not think I can use it to-night. I must consult my husband.

LIV. How you spoil him.

MRS. P. And if we cannot go we will return it by four o'clock. How charmingly your sister did the honours last night.

LIV. She is going to give a concert. Do you like music?

MRS. P. Yes, greatly. (*aside*) When I am *en toilette*. (*aloud*) Are *you* fond of music?

LIV. I'm not afraid of it, but I have something nearer at heart than that at the present moment.

MRS. P. Indeed!

LIV. Yes, I am come to beseech your friendship.

MRS. P. You already have it.

LIV. But there are grades in friendship, and I wish to be ranked as colonel at once.

MRS. P. The first promotion is to an ensigncy.

LIV. Oh, but I have admired you so long.

MRS. P. This was the burden of your song last night at the ball.

LIV. Oh, a ball room is neutral ground where gallantry is part of the programme, and circulates with the refreshments.

MRS. P. You refreshed yourself considerably.

LIV. It was half in jest; but this morning I am very serious, and during the night I have dreamed a dream.

MRS. P. Tell it me?

LIV. The friendship of a woman! That communion of hearts, which possesses all the delicacies of love, without its perfidies; an absolute confidence, which, however, need not exclude a little dash of coquetry, a complete devotion, without despotism, or jealousy; a community where each contributes his, and her, choicest, and in a word, a bond of union without remorse for the woman, or weariness for the man.

MRS. P. What an enchanting dream.

LIV. Why should it not become a reality?

MRS. P. Would you always be satisfied with the rôle of "friend" in this interesting drama?

LIV. What more would there be to desire?

MRS. P. Everything that should be refused!

LIV. But if one asked nothing?

MRS. P. Would one always remain so diffident?

LIV. The moment one should be presumptuous the compact would be dissolved. Will you make the trial?

Mrs. P. (*giving him her hands, which he seizes*) I will.

Liv. It is sworn!

Mrs. P. It is sworn!

Liv. Then I commence my duties at once. I learned yesterday that my dear friend is in some embarrassment.

Mrs. P. I! not the least in the world.

Liv. So! a want of confidence already; then I, with a man's proverbial roughness, boldly break the ice. You have a bill of £300 to meet to-day.

Mrs. P. Who has told you that?

Liv. It suffices that I know it.

Mrs. P. (*with hesitation*) Is it possible that Mr. Duval could have——

Liv. No, madame.

Mrs. P. Now for a little frankness from you. Do you suppose the sum he was trying to obtain yesterday was for me?

Liv. Frankly, I do.

Mrs. P. (*coldly*) Then you are mistaken. I have no debts, and if I had, Mr. Duval has not the slightest right to pay them.

Liv. (*aside*) She evidently attaches some importance to my good opinion of her. (*aloud*) I am happy to have been deceived, madame, but I shall watch my opportunity to serve you.

Mrs. P. I absolve you from your self-imposed task.

Enter Charlotte.

Char. Madame, someone wants to speak to you.

Mrs. P. (*to* Livingstone, *coldly*) I regret, Mr. Livingstone——

Liv. No ceremony with friends—dismiss me. (*he salutes, and as he is disappearing*)

Mrs. P. (*with vivacity*) Mr. Frederic, Mr. Livingstone.

Liv. (*quickly turning*) Madame!

Mrs. P. (*hesitating*) We part friends. (*giving her hand, which he takes and kisses*)

Liv. More friends than ever! (*Exit*)

Char. (*entering*) She has come, ma'am.

Mrs. P. So I supposed. Let us put these things out of sight. (*they hide packages*)

Char. Needn't be afraid, ma'am, if she does know we have to go to my uncle's; he sees some of the best society in town, I'm thinkin'.

Mrs. P. Let her come in.

Enter MADAME ANGELIQUE.

MAD. Well, Mrs. Prendergast, you know what I want.

MRS. P. My dear Madame Angélique, I must get you to renew the bill.

MAD. Not if I know it!

MRS. P. Well, at least, as matters stand, you will take some of the lace back.

MAD. Also, not if I know it, only more so. "Business is business," and once sold is always sold.

MRS. P. Give me till to-morrow?

MAD. Not a minute later than two to-day. I've got a payment to make myself.

CHARLOTTE *enters.*

CHAR. What a Juggernaut! she makes me feel quite faint, a-riding over mistress like that.

MRS. P. Well, it is not two o'clock-yet.

MAD. It isn't far off, and I don't know how £300 is going to spring up out o' the carpet; but for the life of me I can't see what you've got to make such a bother about it. One little scene with your husband and it's all over, and if you don't speak to him, I will; anyway, I don't quit this room till I'm paid.

MRS. P. Well, we will leave you in possession for a little while. Come, Charlotte, it is useless to appeal to her feelings.

CHAR. Yes, ma'am. Feelings! (*they go out in the direction where they left the packages*)

MAD. Feelings! feelings in my trade! why, I should be bankrupt every week. I suppose they're gone to my uncle's! Well, where they like, so they get the money, though I ain't afraid. (*looking round*) Carpets, curtains, furniture, ornaments, all good. He can pay me, poor dear man, and he shall.

Enter PRENDERGAST, GOSLING, *and* AMANDA.

PREN. It was inexcusable in me to leave the papers here, Mr. Gosling; but I do a great deal of work at home, and—— (*sees* MADAME ANGELIQUE)

MAD. I'm waiting for Mrs. Prendergast, sir. I have an appointment with her.

PREN. Very good; pray be seated.

GOS. Oh, I don't mind the trouble; and Mandie wants to see the paper, the—what d' ye call it?

PREN. The deed of gift.

GOS. Deed o' gift. She don't think the house is hers ill she see it on paper. Though I don't know as I ought to give her a house ; she never gives me one. But, however, if she wasn't to get it, perhaps young Mr. Greenway 'd slip through her fingers.

AM. Papa ! how can you talk so ? You know the attachment is sincere and mutual.

GOS. I can't believe as ever *he* asked *you*, Mandie. I never met a man with so few part o' speech in my life. You must have proposed to him, Mandie ; and then his " Yes, Miss Amanda," settled the question—the innocent young lamb !

PREN. Come, come, Mr. Gosling, you are putting Miss Amanda to confusion.

AM. I must try and bear, it Mr. Prendergast, though it does try my too sensitive nature ; but all my efforts are vain. I shall never rear papa !

GOS. Don't you try, dearie; let your old father cackle on just as he likes. *I* never interfe e with other folks's grammar and broughtings up ; then why don't others let me alone ? Fair's fair, and that's all I asks. Grammar rankles in my constitooshuns. *I* don't rankle in other people's constitooshuns, so let me alone, and do as you'd be done by !

PREN. Upon my word I think your father right, Miss Amanda.

AM. Well, perhaps he is, and when I'm young Mrs. Greenway I'll give him up, and leave him to complete his education himself. (*Exit* PRENDERGAST)

GOS. The sensiblest thing as you've said for years, Mandie! And when you're young Mrs. Greenway, your happy old dad'll be cock-o'the-walk again.

PREN. (*entering*) Here is the precious document ; you can take it home, read it at your leisure, and make another appointment with me to sign.

GOS. Good ! as clear as day. Come along, Mandie. Good morning, Mr. Prendergast, good morning. (*salute and exit*)

PREN. (*returning, and taking a ring from his pocket*) 'Tis pretty if simple, and I trust it may be considered a peace offering, as well as a birthday present. My heart smote me for my cruel suspicions of her last night, and my constrained manner this morning. There must be peace between us. I wish she would return. (*as he is going into his study,* MADAME ANGELIQUE, *who, during this time, has been sitting unobserved in a corner of the room, rises as the clock strikes two, and calls him*)

MAD. Mr. Prendergast !

PREN. Well, ma'am, what do you wish ?

MAD. The settlement of this bill, which your wife promised to pay positively to-day at two o'clock. She is not

here, and I concluded I'd better apply to you ; the amount
is £300.

PREN. (*astonished, but pleased*) This, then, is the explanation of her extravagance. (*takes account ; begins reading*)
Fifty pounds for a dress ! What an abomination !

MAD. The price, nevertheless !

PREN. For you, perhaps, but not for me. I shall have this
bill examined before I pay you.

MAD. And I insist on being paid at once. Mrs. Prendergast is satisfied with the price, and if you drive me to law
it will only cost you more, for I've had actions of this kind
before, and I always win, so in addition to paying, you will
have a lot of publicity. I know my points.

PREN. What is your point here ?

MAD. A husband can always be made to pay his wife's
debts, if they are in keeping with his income, and you must
have at least £1200 a year ; anyway, if you haven't, you
spend it.

PREN. (*astounded*) I spend it !

MAD. Every copper of it, or if you don't your wife does.
Why, I could get judgment on the strength of this very
furniture.

PREN. Which is all second-hand.

MAD. I know all about that second-hand dodge. What
do you suppose these chimney ornaments cost you? £5
perhaps. I'll give you £15 cash down, and this carpet, these
curtains, all the whole lot, equally good ; and then your
dinners, your parties, your theatres, your hired carriages.
Oh, I've got my eyes open, I have, and I make it my business to know all about the husbands before I trust the wives.

PREN. (*much agitated*) For aught you know my wife may
have other debts besides yours, and that may account for all
you speak of.

MAD. She must have a pretty good lot then ! In a word,
whether you are rich or poor, I must and will be paid, and
that at once.

PREN. You shall ! you shall !, Say not another word.
(*writes cheque*)

MAD. Ah ! I thought we should understand each other.
All right. (*as she is signing receipt enter* MRS. PRENDERGAST)

MRS. P. My husband ! (PRENDERGAST *exchanges cheque for
receipted bill.* MADAME ANGELIQUE *exit.* PRENDERGAST
approaches slowly to MRS. PRENDERGAST ; *gives her bill, and
after a short silence*)

PREN. I do not reproach you. I am as much to blame as
you are. I should have lent to your youth the sense and
reason of my age. Instead of teaching you order and economy,

I have encouraged your gaieties, but I hoped your good sense would keep you within bounds. I ought to have foreseen all this. I have wanted prudence, you have not given me your confidence. Let us forget our reciprocal wrongs, forget the past, and occupy ourselves with the future, and to that end, give me a list of your creditors. (*he seats himself, and takes a pen and paper*)

MRS. P. My creditors! I have none.

PREN. I am laying no trap for you, my child; but the scene with that woman must not be renewed; so, whatever the amount of your debts, let me know them exactly.

MRS. P. I assure you——

PREN. Do not be afraid. If we are ruined, you will hear no complaint from me. Let me know all, and I will work with a light heart, that you shall not suffer too much for your follies.

MRS. P. If I owed anything I would tell you at once, but I do not.

PREN. (*much moved*) You do not?

MRS. P. No, that bill was my only debt.

PREN. In Heaven's name, be sincere, Cecilia. I cannot understand your obstinacy.

MRS. P. Nor I yours. I'm sure I can't invent debts to please you.

PREN. (*in great agitation*) Will you swear by the memory of your mother?

MRS. P. Good gracious! how solemn you are all of a sudden.

PREN. You dare not!

MRS. P. By the memory of my mother, I swear I owe nothing. There! (PRENDERGAST *staggers back into a chair; she runs towards him*)

PREN. (*hoarsely*) Do not come near me!

MRS. P. (*aside*) Eleanor must have told him.

PREN. I have never refused to gratify your caprices even. I have spent my days in labour to secure your comforts, my strength, my time, my life, all, I have given, and my reward is to have my name associated with that of an abandoned woman. Who has paid for your luxuries, infamous creature, speak? What have you made of me? an accomplice of your shame. Oh, I am not ridiculous, I am dishonoured!

MRS. P. Have mercy upon me, I knew not what I did; Do not overwhelm me. I do not attempt to justify myself! it is for you to decide my fate.

PREN. I must first know his name.

MRS. P. (*quickly*) You did not know it?

PREN. Should I be here now? His name! his name!

Mrs. P. Oh, if any expiation be possible, name it and, whatever the punishment, I will accept it with gratitude.

Pren. First, his name—his name, that I may pay him.

Mrs. P. Pay him?

Pren. If it be my last coin.

Mrs. P. (*with an entire change of manner*) In that case what is to become of us?

Pren. We will work; we may be straitened, but we shall not be indigent. You spoke of expiation—it will commence then.

Mrs. P. Poverty! Oh! I cannot consent.

Pren. Wretched woman, does honest poverty frighten you?

Mrs. P. It does! it does! (*her eyes sinking*).

Pren. I have rescued her from obscurity; and the daily bread which would satisfy me is not enough for her.

Mrs. P. (*bitterly*) You reproach me with your benefactions.

Pren. I reproach myself with having thought you worthy of them.

Mrs. P. (*in a low voice*) If I had been rich I should not have married.

Pren. Monster of perversity!

Mrs. P. Enough of insults! Either leave me or kill me. What could you expect of me? Who ever taught me anything? What was my own mother's maxim? That to be happy you must be rich. What have I learned in the world? That you must be rich to be thought anything of. Pleasure and luxury, money, jewels, dresses, are the gods I have been taught to worship, both by word and example; and because I do worship them, because I *would* have them, I am a monster! A monster be it! Let it end! I am tired of my false life. You are not satisfied with me; turn me out of your house, then. Let it end! I say, let it end!

Pren. (*thunderstruck*) Yes, let it end. You are at home here, madame; and I leave this house never to return. Act henceforth as your instincts prompt you. (*Exit*)

QUICK CURTAIN.

ACT V.

SCENE—DUVAL'S *house.* *Ten o'clock in the evening.* MR. *and* MRS. DUVAL *discovered.*

DUV. Eleanor !

MRS. D. (*wearily*) Well.

DUV. Read this. (*gives her* MRS. PRENDERGAST'S *letter*)

MRS. D. (*reading*) "Your wife knows all! Adieu!—CECILIA."

DUV. You will never forgive me ?

MRS. D. Never.

DUV. And yet you said nothing.

MRS. D. Why should I ? was it not enough that *my* existence should be sacrificed ? I preferred not to break his.

DUV. What a heart you have !

MRS. D. I am an honest woman—nothing more, and I accuse you of accomplishing Cecilia's fall by means of her intimacy here, where everything should have been a safe-guard for her. I accuse you of abusing my confidence, in promoting your friendship with my friend. You, upon whom I would have relied as upon myself to protect her honour !

DUV. Eleanor !

MRS. D. Language fails me to tell you what I think of you, what you have done appears to me so vile.

DUV. I submit to your reproofs almost with satisfaction ; you are but saying to me aloud what I have long been whis-pering to myself. I do not hope to regain your esteem. I have fallen to her level ; I can never hope to rise again to yours. Whatever your wish it shall be obeyed ; I will go or remain, as you decide ; your remembrance or your presence will chastise me equally.

MRS. D. You loved her ?

DUV. I ! If you have been jealous of my heart, be so no longer.

MRS. D. I am not. My pride would prevent that, but it is not a question of hearts. I am more revolted than moved by this double outrage, this betrayal of wife and friend, and you will understand how thoroughly we are sundered, you and I, when I tell you that I pity him more than myself. I do not expect every one to feel for him the friendship and gratitude that fills my soul, but whose heart would *not* bleed at the sight of this wreck, for you have not only wounded the husband in robbing him of his wife, but you have struck down and trailed in mire the dignity of the man. This I will never pardon you, and as long as he lives I will never forget it ! Oh, may a pitying Heaven blind him to the end, for I tell you plainly, Alfred Duval, that if ever the moment comes for me to choose between him and you, I would not hesitate a moment.

Duv. Take care that your "gratitude" does not cause you to forget your duty.

Mrs. D. Is it for you to indicate the boundary line of "duty?"

Duv. Eleanor, you forget there is a living bond between us, our child.

Mrs. D. He who brought me up can be a father to him.

Duv. Eleanor!

John *enters.*

John. Mr. Livingstone, sir.

Duv. Livingstone, at this time of night!

Mrs. D. Let him come in; he may have news. I will leave you together for a while.   (*Exit*)

Enter Livingstone.

Duv. You, Livingstone, at this time?

Liv. Myself! Mr. Prendergast—is he here?

Duv. No. Why?—why?

Liv. I breathe again; but that he *will* come there's no doubt. I come to warn you that he knows all, save and except the name of the lover. So, when you see him, keep your counsel, and your countenance, too, if you can.

Duv. The lover!

Liv. (*echoing*) The lover! Bah! the hour is past for affectation and innocence, my poor fellow. Here is the plain and ugly truth. The magazine has exploded, some second-hand lady's dressmaker applied the torch, and Prendergast's household gods are scattered to the four winds of Heaven; he himself has left his home, never to return.

Duv. The last blow is struck!

Liv. (*drily, and aside*) Perhaps not. (*aloud*) I expect he is as yet unaware it is you. Therefore, try and not betray yourself, if only to secure your wife from the horrors of the *exposé.*

Duv. It is too late! She knows all!

Liv. So much the worse! The devil fly away with all pretty petticoats brought up under the shadow of large incomes by mothers who haven't a shilling. The plot thickens.

Duv. But from whom did you learn it all?

Liv. From the shepherdess herself!

Duv. From Cecilia?

Liv. From Cecilia!

Duv. When?

LIV. To-night.

DUV. To-night! Where did you see her to-night?

LIV. At the Opera.

DUV. At the Opera!

LIV. Even so. A little precipitate perhaps, a trifle disregardless possibly, but then the poor dear thing has never made any special study of etiquette, and probably she dared not stay at home, with only her own thoughts for company.

DUV. The theatre at such a crisis as this! What must she be made of?

LIV. Make no wonder of it. I find it the most natural thing in the world. For if she has to think, better do it with other people's thoughts, for a time at least. As soon as I had gathered the story I rushed off to put you on your guard—hence my late visit. And now, a man warned is two men, so you two think it out.

DUV. What is to be done?

LIV. Women are the best counsellors, and since your wife has nothing more to learn of the matter, ask her advice.

DUV. (*after a little hesitation*) You are right. Eleanor! (*he opens her door; she returns*)

MRS. D. Well?

DUV. Summon all your fortitude.

MRS. D. What new misfortune? speak!

LIV. In a word, then, Mr. Prendergast has discovered all; and I came to inform you that he has left his house, never to set foot in it again.

MRS. D. At last! at last! unhappy man!

LIV. (*with hesitation*) I have further to say that the name —the name of—of——

MRS. D. My husband? (*bitterly*)

LIV. Has not been uttered.

MRS. D. If this be so, why is Mr. Prendergast not here? Here—where he is sure that one heart beats faithfully for him.

LIV. I assure you——

MRS. D. You have seen him?

LIV. No, but I accidentally met Mrs. Prendergast.

MRS. D. Where? where? I too must see, must speak with her.

DUV. How? you would——

MRS. D. For his sake I would; he must be spared. Tell me, Mr. Livingstone, where I can find her?

LIV. I would rather not tell you.

DUV. (*suddenly*) She is at the Opera.

MRS. D. (*astounded*) Heartless! hopeless!

The door opens and PRENDERGAST *is seen entering.*

LIV. (*excitedly*) Mr. Prendergast!

MRS. D. Ah!

All three remain motionless as PRENDERGAST *enters.*

PREN. (*walking with difficulty and utterly broken down*) It is I, my dear friends. I see by your faces that you know all. (*he comes down slowly*) For thirty years be the artisan of your own honour, the builder up of your good name, and then——I have walked all the evening and am broken down with fatigue. (LIVINGSTONE *puts a chair for him to sit*) It must be very late.

MRS. D. No.

PREN. (*to* MRS. DUVAL) Yes, my child, Cecilia has dishonoured your poor old guardian; she sold herself to a lover. There are such wives, it seems, and mine was one of the number! I saw nothing of it, suspected nothing! nothing shook my confidence or disturbed my belief in my happiness, and even at this supreme moment I can scarcely believe it. But it is beyond doubt! beyond doubt! (*rising, and with more animation*) But you will aid me, will you not, in discovering her accomplice? I must return his money, the money he has spent upon me and mine; for till I have done this I shall know no peace. Can I rest till I have cast his accursed money in his traitorous face! Can I rest till I have found this man who has slain my honour and broken my heart!

MRS. D. You break mine to hear you talk so; but bear up against this first shock, and time shall heal the wound. (*as she moves towards him, he sees* DUVAL, *who has till then been partly concealed by his wife*)

PREN. Ah! good evening, Alfred. I did not see you. Oh! if they knew the enormity of the evil they do, these corrupters of women! There, there, I will try and bear up, my child. You will have a room prepared for me, for tonight, will you not? only for to-night, for I know not where else to go, and I am almost exhausted, body as well as soul.

MRS. D. (*startled*) Here! (*aside*)

PREN. Eleanor, who told you?

MRS. D. I—Charlotte—she——

PREN. Where did you see her?

MRS. D. John met her in the street.

PREN. Yes, that may be so, for she is not at the house. Foolish old man that I am, I could not resist passing under her windows once more; there was no light; I trembled— perhaps she—I rang the bell in my fright; no one answered, but the servant next door said, "Mrs. Prendergast is gone to the theatre, and Charlotte is out." I was not surprised; nothing astonishes me now.

MRS. D. (*resting his head on her bosom*) **Father**!

LIV. My dear Mr. Prendergast, bear this misfortune like a man ; it is only a misfortune, for shame, like crime, is personal, and what is *your* shame ?

PREN. My wife's.

LIV. She ceased to be your wife the moment she was false to her wifely duties.

PREN. Then I am afraid I have long been wifeless. A hundred things recur to me that I thought nothing of at the time. Do you remember telling us of that carriage being upset in Piccadilly, and the two occupants escaping ? Did you notice how interested she was in your account of it ? She was the woman, I am now convinced.

LIV. Why should you think that ?

PREN. It was she, it was she !

MRS. D. (*aside*) I tremble.

PREN. Eleanor, on your honour, did you suspect nothing ?

MRS. D. (*much agitated*) I !

PREN. Alfred, you who saw so much of her ?

LIV. To-morrow, to-morrow, Mr. Prendergast ; you will not be so excited to-morrow ; let us talk further on the matter then.

PREN. Be it so, be it so, but "out of the fulness of the heart the mouth speaketh,"—to-morrow, Eleanor, I will take some rooms in the neighbourhood ; for to-night you will let me sleep here will——

LIV. Better come with me. I have always a guest chamber ready, and I shall be happy to have you with me, and then we need not disturb Mrs. Duval ; it may not be quite convenient, perhaps—come !

PREN. Will my stopping here for [a single night disturb you, Eleanor ?

MRS. D. Yes—no—that is—I——

PREN. You have not a corner to give me ; shall I ask in vain in *your* house ? This arm chair will serve me ; 'tis but for one night. Why do you lower your eyes ? What is the matter ? You are all embarrassed, it seems to me ; what is it ? (*aside to* MRS. DUVAL) Perhaps Alfred objects. (*aloud to* DUVAL) Do not separate me from her, from my Eleanor, now, Alfred, my friend, my son. (*he opens his arms and moves towards* DUVAL, *as if to throw them appealingly round him.* MRS. DUVAL *by an instinctive movement stops him;* PRENDERGAST *stops astonished, looks from one to another, all intensely agitated ; then a light seems to break in upon him, his face expresses horror, and he exclaims to* DUVAL) It was you ! (*he rushes towards him, his arm uplifted;* MRS. DUVAL *and* LIVINGSTONE *intercept him*)

MRS. D. He is my husband !

LIV. Spare *her* ! *She* is innocent !

PREN. The blow has reached my heart ! (*he sinks on a chair,*
MRS. DUVAL *supporting him*) You can pardon him, Eleanor,
for the world's verdict will be that *his* honour is unsoiled ;
while mine !—while mine ! (*covers his face with his hands*)

DUV. Eleanor ! Mr. Prendergast ! What reparation can
I make ?

MRS. D. (*rising to her full height*) I am your judge !
Hear my sentence. I told you that when the moment came
for me to choose between you and him, I should not hesitate.
It has come, and my resolution is taken. For years you
have been the lord of my heart. I tear you from it ! Go !
and compare your gain with your loss. You have bought
the fleeting affections of a wanton ; you have sacrificed, and
for ever, the true love of a true woman, and as loyal a
friendship as ever man gave to man. Look at your work !
Two crushed lives, and two broken households ! Never hope
or think to see me again ; our lives, as our hearts, are no
longer one, but twain ; for the present has killed the past—
the future, too ; and henceforth you and I shall know each
other no more. To-day Eleanor Duval's wifehood terminates
for ever, and she exists but as mother—and— (*sinking on
her knees by* PRENDERGAST'S *chair ; he places his hand on her
head*) daughter !

PREN. My child ! My child !

DUV. (*rushing forward*) Eleanor !

LIV. (*to him*) Not a word now ! Leave Time **and me to**
try and make your peace.

Curtain.

www.ingramcontent.com/pod-product-compliance
Lightning Source LLC
Chambersburg PA
CBHW021236260626
47172CB00002B/788